EXCUSE ME, HAVE YOU SEEN A FLASHING LIGHT?

BOOK ISLAND
BERNARDO CARVALHO

EXCUSE ME,
HAVE YOU SEEN
A FLASHING
LIGHT?

FOLLOW THE FIREFLY!

BOOK ISLAND

RUN, RABBIT, RUN!

FOLLOW THE RABBIT!

BERNARDO CARVALHO

This edition first published in 2014
by Book Island, New Zealand
info@bookisland.co.nz

Text & illustrations © Bernardo Carvalho 2013
English language edition © Book Island 2014

Original titles:
1. *Olhe, por favor, não viu uma luzinha a piscar?*
2. *Corre, coelhinho, corre!*
© Editora Planeta Tangerina, Portugal 2013

A catalogue record for this book is available
from the National Library of New Zealand.

Edited by Frith Williams

The publication of this book has been funded by
the General Directorate for Books, Archives and Libraries in Portugal.

GOVERNO DE
PORTUGAL

SECRETÁRIO DE ESTADO
DA CULTURA

ISBN: 978 0 9941098 2 8

Visit **www.bookisland.co.nz** for more information about our titles.

BOOK ISLAND